LITTLE ELEPHANT

By JESSICA POTTER BRODERICK

Illustrated by LUCY OZONE

RAND McNALLY & COMPANY • Chicago

Established 1856

LITTLE ELEPHANT lay on the
ground. Slowly he opened his
eyes. It was early morning and
dew sparkled on the grass. Little
Elephant could hear the soft
rumbling in his mother's throat,

and he could see his father, a huge elephant with long white tusks, leaning against an acacia tree, fast asleep.

Then Little Elephant felt his

mother nudging him with her strong, gentle trunk.

"Get up, Little Elephant," she said. "This is your birthday! You are four years old."

Little Elephant rolled over and stood up. He *was* growing big! His baby pink color had long ago disappeared, also the black fuzz that had covered his back and forehead.

"Come along, Little One,"
said his mother. "We are going
for a birthday walk to see our
friends and, at the end of the
walk, there will be a wonderful
surprise!"

As Little Elephant and his mother went along they saw a giraffe eating leaves from the top of a mimosa tree.

"Good morning, Giraffe," said Mother Elephant. "This is Little Elephant's birthday."

"Happy birthday, Little Elephant," said the giraffe.

Next they saw a fat hippo-
potamus sticking his head up out
of the river.

"Good morning, Hippopota-mus," said Mother Elephant. "This is Little Elephant's birth-day."

"Happy birthday, Little Ele-phant," snorted the hippopota-mus.

When they walked under a
mahogany tree, they saw a monkey swinging by his tail.

"Hello, Monkey," said Mother
Elephant. "This is Little Elephant's birthday."

"Happy birthday, Little Elephant," chattered the monkey.
"Here is a present for you." He
threw a banana down onto the
ground.

"Thank you, Monkey," said Little Elephant. He picked up the banana with his tiny trunk and ate it. He had never tasted anything so delicious.

"And now for the surprise!" said Mother Elephant. "It's just over this hill."

Little Elephant was so eager
to get up the hill he grabbed
hold of his mother's tail and let
her pull him along.

At the top of the hill Little
Elephant looked down and saw
five small elephants playing to-
gether. Each little elephant was
holding another's tail so that

they formed a long line. They were playing Follow the Leader.

"This is the surprise," said Mother Elephant. "Today you are big enough to learn to play with the others."

Little Elephant scrambled down the hill and took his place at the end of the line. He ran about with the small elephants as they moved around and be-

hind the trees. Then they danced
a Ring around the Orchid.

After a while Mother Ele-
phant called Little Elephant to
her. "You have learned to play
very well," she said. "Now you

are ready for a *big* surprise. Follow me."

She led Little Elephant up-
stream to a spot where other
small elephants were sliding down

a mossy slope into the river.

This time Little Elephant stayed close to his mother's side. The bank looked *very* steep to him. He wasn't at all sure he wanted to slide down it.

"Go on, Small One," said Mother Elephant. She gave him a shove with her forehead.

Whee-ee-ee-ee!—away went Little Elephant down the slope and SPLASH! into the water.

"Why, that was fun!" shrilled
Little Elephant. "I want to do it
again!"

So he *did* do it again, and
again—and again—and *again*.

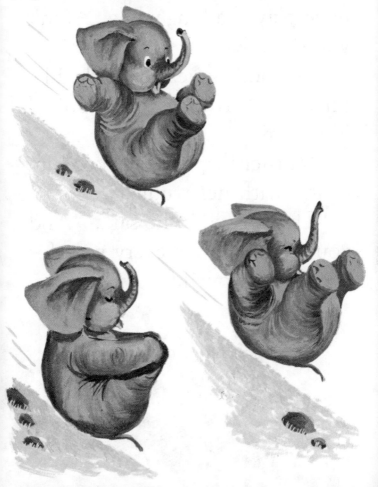

"Come here, Little One," said Mother Elephant at last. "You have played a long while. Aren't you tired?"

"Oh no," squealed Little Elephant. "Birthdays are fun! I *like* them!"

Mother Elephant stroked him gently with her trunk.

"That's good," she said. "And you will have one every year for the rest of your life."